Lauren's moving Day

By Sarah, Duchess of York

Illustrated by Ian Cunliffe

STERLING CHILDREN'S BOOKS

New York

STERLING CHILDREN'S BOOKS
New York

An Imprint of Sterling Publishing
387 Park Avenue South
New York, NY 10016

STERLING and the distinctive Sterling logo are registered trademarks of
Sterling Publishing Co., Inc.

Library of Congress Cataloging-in-Publication Data Available

Lot#:
2 4 6 8 10 9 7 5 3 1
03/11
Published by Sterling Publishing Co., Inc.
387 Park Avenue South, New York, NY 10016
www.sterlingpublishing.com/kids
Story and illustrations © 2007 by Startworks Ltd.
"Ten Helpful Hints" © 2009 by Startworks Ltd.
Distributed in Canada by Sterling Publishing
c/o Canadian Manda Group, 165 Dufferin Street
Toronto, Ontario, Canada M6K 3H6
Distributed in Australia by Capricorn Link (Australia) Pty. Ltd.
P.O. Box 704, Windsor, NSW 2756, Australia

Sterling ISBN 978-1-4027-7398-3

For information about custom editions, special sales, premium and
corporate purchases, please contact Sterling Special Sales
Department at 800-805-5489 or specialsales@sterlingpublishing.com.

All children face many new experiences as they grow up, and helping them to understand and deal with each is one of the most demanding and rewarding things we do as parents. Helping Hand Books are for both children and parents to read, perhaps together. Each simple story describes a childhood experience and shows some of the ways in which to make it a positive one. I do hope these books encourage children and parents to talk about these sometimes difficult issues. Talking together goes a long way to finding a solution.

Sarah,

Sarah, Duchess of York

Lauren woke with a start. She had a funny feeling and, for a moment, she couldn't work out why.

Then she remembered. Today was the day: the day of her family's big move.

Lauren knew that she should feel excited. Her mom had taken her to see the new house lots of times, and it looked very nice. Lauren was going to have her own bedroom for the first time, and the backyard was big enough to play hide-and-seek in.

Lauren was excited, but she had another feeling, too. She was anxious.

What would it be like to live in another house? she thought. Lauren lay in bed listening to all the sounds she knew well: the traffic in the street, the bird in the tree outside her window, and the neighbor's dog, Max, barking at the clouds. She felt anxious and worried. Everything was going to change.

All of Lauren's things were already packed. Poking out of one of the moving boxes was her favorite teddy bear, Button.

"Don't worry, Button," said Lauren, jumping out of bed. "I know moving feels strange, but we still have each other. Being together is what really matters."

That morning, Lauren ate breakfast while sitting on top of a box. She had to eat her cereal with a fork because everything else had been packed!

After breakfast, the phone rang. It was Lauren's best friend, Madison, calling to wish her good luck with the move.

"I want to hear all about your move," said Madison. "You are so lucky to have a real-life adventure. Don't forget about our playdate next week!"

Lauren didn't really want to have a real-life adventure. She would rather things stayed exactly the same.

As she hung up the phone, the doorbell rang. It was Stan, "The Man with the Van." He had come to help Lauren's family move their things to the new house.

Stan and his movers worked most of the morning. Finally everything was packed up in the van.

Lauren and her mom took
one last look around the house.
It was empty and didn't seem at
all like the house they had loved.
"Come on!" said Mom.
"Let's go to our new house.
We'll start putting your things
in your new room."

The new house also looked empty at first. But as the movers began to unload all their furniture and belongings, everything started to look more familiar.

Stan was carrying a large box upstairs when he tripped. Button fell out, bumping his head on the stairs. Lauren rushed to pick him up.

"Poor Button!" she said reassuringly. "Sit here in the kitchen until we are more settled."

Lauren had helped her mom put labels on every box and piece of furniture so that Stan knew where everything belonged. It was surprising how quickly the house began to look like a home.

"First things first," said Lauren's mom. "Let's sort your room out."

Before the move, Lauren and her mom had spent a long time planning where everything would go in her new room. They had even gone to the store to buy new wallpaper and matching curtains. Lauren got to choose everything!

All of Lauren's things fit perfectly in her room. Lauren heard her stuffed animals squabble about who would go on the bed and who had to go on the shelf. Button, of course, went in his usual place of honor on Lauren's pillow.

Just after Stan, "The Man with the Van," left, the doorbell rang again. Lauren and her mom opened the door and saw two boys standing on the front porch. One looked a little older than Lauren and one looked a little younger.

"Hi, my name is Jack," said the older boy. "And this is my brother, Tommy. We live next door. We saw your moving van and wanted to say hello."

"And to see if you want to play," added Tommy excitedly.

"How nice of you," said Lauren's mom. "Lauren, you may go play for half an hour. It has been a long day, so be back soon."

Lauren went outside with Jack and Tommy. She was thrilled to find out that Jack had the same bike as she had, just in a different color. The three of them had fun together, and Lauren was happy she had made some new friends.

That night, Lauren was back in the new house and snuggled up in her new bedroom. The day had gone so fast and so had her real-life adventure.

As Lauren lay in bed, she listened to the new noises around her. They already started sounding familiar. This new house was going to be okay after all.

Lauren turned to Button and said, "I think our new house is going to feel like home before we know it. What do you think?"

But Button was already fast asleep!

TEN HELPFUL HINTS

TO PREPARE YOUR CHILD FOR MOVING TO A NEW HOME

By Dr. Richard Woolfson, PhD

1. Give your child advance warning. Moving is a big change for everyone, especially your child. A change of environment can be scary, and she won't know what to expect. Explain the situation in advance so that she has time to adjust to the idea of moving.

2. Involve your child in the moving process. Before the move, take your child to the new home and explain why you chose it. Take him around the new neighborhood and point out all the positive things about it.

3. Focus on the positives and advantages of the new home. Highlight the ways in which the new home compares favorably with your existing home—more rooms, better play areas, or a bigger backyard.

4. Give your child some control over her choices, such as how her room will be decorated. Even a young child can be involved in choosing wallpaper, paint, or curtains. Excitement about her choices can help pave the way for acceptance of her new environment.

5. If possible, maintain connections and relationships with old friends and neighbors. Tell your child that he can call them whenever he wants to. If you are not moving far away, make plans for him to see his old friends soon after the move. By doing so, you will reassure him that some things don't have to change because you've moved.

6. Before the move, take your child to her new school. If possible, allow her to meet her new teacher and visit with her new class for an hour or two. This will enable her to build up her self-confidence and familiarity so her first day of school won't feel so strange and new.

7. Before the move, do something to make your child feel extra-special. For example, host a special moving party for your child and his friends a few weeks before the actual move. This will reassure him that he is the most important thing in the world to you and that his feelings are important, too.

8. After the move, make it a priority to get your child's room in order as soon as possible. Put all her bedroom furniture into place and lay out all her favorite toys right away.

9. Keep a young child distracted or out of the house on the day of the move. Going to school or staying with a relative will prevent him from having to face the actual move head-on, which could cause unnecessary anxiety for everyone.

10. Be aware that your child might experience "post-move blues." For a couple of weeks after the move, spend time with your child each day talking to her about her new home. Your young child will need lots of love and attention during this difficult phase. The impact of moving can extend beyond the actual moving day.

Dr. Richard Woolfson is a child psychologist, working with children and their families. He is also an author and has written several books on child development and family life, in addition to numerous articles for magazines and newspapers. Dr. Woolfson runs training workshops for parents and child care professionals and appears regularly on radio and television. He is a Fellow of the British Psychological Society.

Helping Hand Books

Look for these other helpful books to share with your child:

Ashley Learns About Strangers

Emily's First Day of School

Michael and His New Baby Brother

Matthew and the Bullies

When Katie's Parents Separated

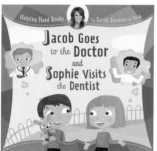

Jacob Goes to the Doctor and Sophie Visits the Dentist

Molly makes Friends

Olivia says Goodbye to Grandpa

Healthy Food for Dylan

Get Well Soon Adam

Zach gets Some Exercise